双语名著无障碍阅读丛书

经典集锦

一个孩子的诗园

A Child's Garden of Verses

[英国] 罗伯特·路易斯·史蒂文森 著

陈冬宁 译　章艳 校译

中国出版集团

中译出版社

图书在版编目（CIP）数据

一个孩子的诗园：英汉对照／（英）罗伯特·路易
斯·史蒂文森著；陈冬宁译. —北京：中译出版社，2019.10
（双语名著无障碍阅读丛书）
ISBN 978-7-5001-6032-8

Ⅰ.①一… Ⅱ.①罗… ②陈… Ⅲ.①英语－汉语－对照读物②儿童
诗歌－诗集－英国－近代 Ⅳ.①H319.4：I

中国版本图书馆CIP数据核字（2019）第188652号

出版发行／中译出版社
地　　址／北京市西城区车公庄大街甲4号物华大厦6层
电　　话／（010）68359827；　68359303（发行部）；　53601537（编辑部）
邮　　编／100044
传　　真／（010）68357870
电子邮箱／book@ctph.com.cn
网　　址／http://www.ctph.com.cn

总 策 划／张高里　贾兵伟
策划编辑／胡晓凯
责任编辑／范祥镇

封面设计／潘　峰
排　　版／北京竹页文化传媒有限公司

经　　销／新华书店

规　　格／710毫米×1000毫米　1/16
印　　张／11.75
字　　数／46千字
版　　次／2019年10月第一版
印　　次／2019年10月第一次

ISBN 978-7-5001-6032-8　定价：25.00元

多年以来，中译出版社有限公司（原中国对外翻译出版有限公司）凭借国内一流的翻译和出版实力及资源，精心策划、出版了大批双语读物，在海内外读者中和业界内产生了良好、深远的影响，形成了自己鲜明的出版特色。

二十世纪八九十年代出版的英汉（汉英）对照"一百丛书"，声名远扬，成为一套最权威、最有特色且又实用的双语读物，影响了一代又一代英语学习者和中华传统文化研究者、爱好者；还有"英若诚名剧译丛""中华传统文化精粹丛书""美丽英文书系"，这些优秀的双语读物，有的畅销，有的常销不衰反复再版，有的被选为大学英语阅读教材，受到广大读者的喜爱，获得了良好的社会效益和经济效益。

"双语名著无障碍阅读丛书"是中译专门为中学生和英语学习者精心打造的又一品牌，是一个新的双语读物系列，具有以下特点：

选题创新——该系列图书是国内第一套为中小学生量身打造的双语名著读物，所选篇目均为教育部颁布的语文新课标必读书目，或为中学生以及同等文化水平的社会读者喜闻乐见的世界名著，重新编译为英汉（汉英）对照的双语读本。这些书既给青少年读者提供了成长过程中不可或缺的精神食粮，又让他们领略到原著的精髓和魅力，对他们更好地学习英文大有裨益；同时，丛书中入选的《论语》《茶馆》《家》等汉英对照读物，亦是热爱中国传统文化的中外读者所共知的经典名篇，能使读者充分享受阅读经典的无限乐趣。

无障碍阅读——中学生阅读世界文学名著的原著会遇到很多生词和文化难点。针对这一情况，我们给每一本读物原文中的较难词汇和不易理解之处都加上了注释，在内文的版式设计上也采取英汉（或汉英）对照方式，扫清了学生阅读时的障碍。

优良品质——中译双语读物多年来在读者中享有良好口碑，这得益于作者和出版者对于图书质量的不懈追求。"双语名著无障碍阅读丛书"继承了中译双语读物的优良传统——精选的篇目、优秀的译文、方便实用的注解，秉承着对每一个读者负责的精神，竭力打造精品图书。

愿这套丛书成为广大读者的良师益友，愿读者在英语学习和传统文化学习两方面都取得新的突破。

目录
CONTENTS

目
CONTENTS
录

目录
CONTENTS

目录
CONTENTS

目录
CONTENTS

目录
CONTENTS

目录
CONTENTS

Robert Louis Stevenson

To Alison Cunningham

From Her Boy

For the long nights you lay awake
And watched for my unworthy sake:
For your most comfortable hand
That led me through the uneven land:
For all the story-books you read:
For all the pains you comforted:
For all you pitied, all you bore,
In sad and happy days of yore:—
My second Mother, my first Wife,
The angel of my infant life—
From the sick child, now well and old,
Take, nurse, the little book you hold!
And grant it, Heaven, that all who read
May find as dear a nurse at need,
And every child who lists my rhyme,
In the bright, fireside, nursery clime,
May hear it in as kind a voice
As made my childish days rejoice!

R. L. S.

致艾莉森·坎宁安

来自她的乖孩子

感谢你漫漫长夜不合眼，
为了我这个小不点劳烦；
感谢你无限温暖的手，
牵引我走过高低不平的路；
感谢你为我讲一本本故事书；
感谢你一次次抚慰我的痛楚；
感谢你所有的同情所有的忍受，
往昔的日子有喜有忧；
我的第二个妈妈啊，我的第一个妻子，
你是我孩童时期的天使——
当年生病的小孩如今是一个健康的老人，
保姆啊，请收下你手中的这本小书！
上天啊，请让每位读到此书的孩子，
需要时都有亲切的保姆为之守候，
在亮堂堂的育婴室，在炉火旁，
愿每个孩子都有一个仁慈的声音，
为他们朗读我的诗行，
那样的声音让我的童年充满欢畅。

罗伯特·路易斯·史蒂文森

A Child's Garden of Verses

一个孩子的诗园

Bed in Summer

In winter I get up at night
And dress by yellow candle-light.
In summer, quite the other way,
I have to go to bed by day.
I have to go to bed and see
The birds still **hopping** [1] on the tree,
Or hear the **grown-up** [2] people's feet
Still going past me in the street.
And does it not seem hard to you,
When all the sky is clear and blue,
And I should like so much to play,
To have to go to bed by day?

夏天的床

冬天，天不亮我就要起床，
借着黄色的烛光穿衣裳。
夏天，正好和那相反，
睡觉的时候天还很亮。
睡觉的时候还能看到，
树上的鸟儿不停地跳，
还能听见大人的脚步，
来来回回地经过此路。
天空那么晴朗，那么蓝，
我多么希望再玩一玩，
睡觉的时候还是白天，
你说是不是会让我心烦？

① hop [hɔp] v. 双足跳行
② grown-up ['grəun'ʌp] a.
成年的

A Thought

It is very nice to think
The world is full of meat and drink,
With little children saying **grace** [①]
In every Christian kind of place.

奇想

① grace [greis] *n.*（饭前或饭后的）谢恩祷告

这么想想可真美好，
世上到处是美味佳肴，
在每一处信仰基督的地方，
孩子们祈祷把主颂扬。

At the Seaside

When I was down beside the sea
A wooden **spade**^① they gave to me
To dig the sandy shore.
My holes were empty like a cup,
In every hole the sea camp up
Till it could come no more.

在海边

我来到海边，
他们给我一个小木铲，
让我挖沙子。
空空的沙坑就像水杯，
每个杯里都装进海水，
直到潮水终于退去。

Young Night Thought

All night long, and every night,
When my mamma puts out the light,
I see the people **marching** [①] by,
As plain as day [②], before my eye.
Armies and emperors and kings,
All carrying different kinds of things,
And marching in so grand a way,
You never saw the like by day.
So fine a show was never seen
At the great **circus** [③] on the **green** [④];
For every kind of beast and man
Is marching in that **caravan** [⑤].
At first they move a little slow,
But still the faster on they go,
And still beside them close I keep
Until we reach the town of Sleep.

夜里的遐想

① march [mɑːtʃ] v. 行进，行军
② as plain as day 非常清楚

整整一晚上，每天都这样，
妈妈熄灭灯烛时，
我看见行进的队伍，
就像白天一样明亮。
军队、皇帝和国王，
都带着不同的行装，
前进的气势很恢宏，
是白天没有的阵容。
如此精彩的表演

③ circus ['səːkəs] n. 马戏团
④ green [griːn] n.（尤指城镇或村庄中心的）绿地
⑤ caravan ['kærəvæn] n. 大篷车

赛过草坪上的马戏团；
各色的人与兽，
一路往前走。
开始，他们走得有点慢，
但后来加速向前赶。
我在一旁紧紧跟上，
直到最后都抵达梦乡。

Whole Duty of Children

A child should always say what's true,
And speak when he is spoken to,
And behave **mannerly** ① at table:
At least as far as he is able.

孩子们该做的

孩子应该讲真话，
别人叫他要应答，
餐桌礼仪不能丢：
至少勉力去遵守。

① mannerly ['mænəli] *ad.*
　行为端正地

Rain

The rain is raining all around,
It falls on field and tree,
It rains on the umbrellas here,
And on the ships at sea.

雨

到处都在下着雨，
落在田间树木上，
打在这边的雨伞上，
还有航海的船只上。

Pirate① Story

Three of us **afloat**② in the **meadow**③ by the swing,
Three of us aboard in the basket on the **lea**④.
Winds are in the air, they are blowing in the spring,
And waves are on the meadows like the waves
there are at sea.
Where shall we adventure, to-day that we're afloat,
Wary of the weather and **steering**⑤ by a star?
Shall it be to Africa, a-steering of the boat,
To **Providence**⑥, or **Babylon**⑦, or off to **Malabar**⑧?
Hi! But there's a **squadron**⑨ a-rowing on the sea —
Cattle on the meadow a-charging with a roar!
Quick, and we'll escape them, they're as mad as they can be.
The **wicket**⑩ is the harbour and the garden is the shore.

海盗的故事

① pirate ['paiərət] *n.* 海盗
② afloat [ə'fləut] *a.* 漂浮的
③ meadow ['medəu] *n.* 草地
④ lea [li:] *n.* 草地
⑤ steer [stiə] *v.* 引导
⑥ Providence ['prɔvidns] *n.* 普罗维登斯（美国罗得岛州的首府）
⑦ Babylon ['bæbilən] *n.* 巴比伦（古代巴比伦王国的首都）
⑧ Malabar ['mæləbɑ:(r)] *n.* 马拉巴尔海岸
⑨ squadron ['skwɔdrən] *n.* 海军分遣舰队
⑩ wicket ['wikit] *n.* 小门，边门

我们三个在草地上荡着秋千，
我们三个在草地上登上吊篮。
空中阵阵风吹，吹拂在春天。
原野的绿波就像滚滚的海浪。
我们今天漂到哪里探险呢？
留意天象，让星星引航。
去非洲怎么样，驾着飞船，
去普罗维登斯、巴比伦还是马拉巴尔海岸？
看呀！海上的舰队在奋力赛船——
那是草场上的牛群咆哮向前！
快，我们快躲开，它们实在很疯狂。
让我们驶向栅门的港口，回到花园的岸上。

Foreign Lands

Up into the cherry tree
Who should climb but little me?
I held the trunk with both my hands
And looked abroad on foreign lands.
I saw the next-door garden lie,
Adorned with [①] flowers before my eye,
And many pleasant places more
Than I had never seen before.
I saw the **dimpling** [②] river pass
And be the sky's blue **looking-glass** [③];
The dusty roads go up and down
With people **tramping** [④] in to town.
If I could find a higher tree
Farther and farther I should see,
To where the grown-up river slips
Into the sea among the ships,
To where the roads on either hand
Lean onward into fairy land,
Where all the children dine at five,
And all the playthings come alive.

陌生的地方

① adorn with 用……装饰

② dimple ['dimpl] v. 起涟漪

③ looking-glass ['lukiŋ'glæs] n. 镜子

④ tramp [træmp] v. 重步行走

除了我这个小孩，
谁敢爬上樱桃树呢？
用双手抱着树干，
眺望陌生的地方。
我看见邻居的园门，
鲜花装扮得很好看。
更有很多美妙的地方，
我都未曾好好欣赏。
我看见小河淙淙，
映照着蔚蓝的天空；
起伏的路上尘土飞扬，
人们进城的脚步咚咚响。
如果我爬上更高的树，
就能望向更远处，
看江河汇入海洋，
看轮船渡海去远航，
左右两边的道路，
向前通往神奇的国度，
那里的小朋友五点就吃饱喝足，
那里的玩具会唱歌跳舞。

Windy Nights

Whenever the moon and stars are set,
Whenever the wind is high,
All night long in the dark and wet,
A man goes riding by.
Late in the night when the fires are out,
Why does he **gallop**^① and gallop about?
Whenever the trees are crying aloud,
And ships are **tossed**^② at sea,
By, on the highway, low and loud,
By at the gallop goes he.
By at the gallop he goes, and then
By he comes back at the gallop again.

大风之夜

天上星月暗淡，

大风呼呼地吹个不停，

一晚上又暗又潮，

有个人骑马奔跑。

灯火熄灭夜已深，

为什么他还不停地跑？

每当树叶哗哗响，

船儿在海上摇晃，

大路上的马蹄声，时轻时响，

那个人在快马飞奔，

那个人在快马飞奔，

飞奔而去又见他飞奔而回。

① gallop ['gæləp] v. 飞驰

② toss [tɔs] v. 颠簸

Travel

I would like to rise and go
Where the golden apples grow;
Where below another sky
Parrot islands **anchored**[①] lie,
And, watched by **cockatoos**[②] and goats,
Lonely Crusoes building boats;
Where in sunshine reaching out
Eastern cities, miles about,
Are with **mosque**[③] and **minaret**[④]
Among sandy gardens set,
And the rich goods from near and far
Hang for sale in the **bazaar**[⑤];
Where the Great Wall round China goes,
And on one side the desert blows,
And with bell and voice and drum,
Cities on the other hum;
Where are forests, hot as fire,
Wide as England, tall as a **spire**[⑥],
Full of **apes**[⑦] and coco-nuts

旅行

① anchor ['æŋkə] v. 固定
② cockatoo [kɔkə'tu:] n. 凤头鹦鹉

③ mosque [mɔsk] n. 清真寺
④ minaret ['minəret] n. 宣礼塔（塔身细高，常为清真寺的一部分，上有阳台，宣礼者在此召唤教徒做祷告）
⑤ bazaar [bə'zɑ:] n.（中东国家的）集市

⑥ spire ['spaiə] n.【建】尖塔
⑦ ape [eip] n. 猿

我希望起身就前往，
种着金苹果的地方；
那片天空下
鹦鹉岛安了家，
凤头鹦鹉和山羊来旁观，
孤独的鲁滨逊正在造船；
阳光普照东方城邦，
绵延千里伸向八方，
清真寺和宣礼塔，
在大漠庄园的背景下，
各处来的丰富土产，
在集市上悬挂售卖；
万里长城巍巍蜿蜒，
城墙一边沙尘漫天，
另一边的城镇繁忙，
摇铃打鼓人声喧嚷；
火焰般炽热的森林，
像英格兰那么宽广，
像尖塔那么高，

And the **negro** ① hunters' huts;
Where the **knotty** ② crocodile
Lies and blinks in the **Nile** ③,
And the red **flamingo** ④ flies
Hunting fish before his eyes;
Where in jungles, near and far,
Man-**devouring** ⑤ tigers are,
Lying close and giving ear
Lest the hunt be **drawing near** ⑥,
Or a comer-by be seen
Swinging in a **palanquin** ⑦;
Where among the desert sands
Some deserted city stands,
All its children, sweep and prince,
Grown to manhood ages since,
Not a foot in street or house,
Not a **stir** ⑧ of child or mouse,
And when kindly falls the night,
In all the town no spark of light.
There I'll come when I'm a man
With a camel caravan;
Light a fire in the **gloom** ⑨
Of some dusty dining-room;
See the pictures on the walls,
Heroes, fights and festivals;
And in a corner find the toys
Of the old Egyptian boys.

① negro ['niːgrəu] *n.* 黑人
② knotty ['nɔti] *a.* 多瘤的
③ Nile [nail] *n.* 尼罗河
④ flamingo [flə'miŋgəu] *n.*
   火烈鸟

⑤ devour [di'vauə] *v.* 吞食

⑥ draw near 靠近

⑦ palanquin [ˌpælən'kiːn]
   n. 轿子

⑧ stir [stəː] *n.* 微动

⑨ gloom [gluːm] *n.* 昏暗

到处是人猿和椰果，

和黑人猎手的小窝；

满身是节疤的猛鳄，

闭目躺卧在尼罗河，

红火烈鸟奋起飞舞，

把眼前的鱼来追捕；

丛林里，远近各处，

都会有食人的老虎，

凑近躺下仔细听闻，

以防引来打猎的人，

或恐有过路人出现，

轿子一摇一摆向前；

茫茫荒漠的背景下，

废弃之都兀自挺拔，

城中孩子无论贵贱，

早就已经长大成年，

到处都没什么动静，

也没有调皮的身影，

夜幕慢悠悠地下降，

哪都不见一丝光亮。

我长大后要去那里，

骆驼纵队跟着一起；

黑暗之中点火照亮，

原来是尘封的饭堂；

看墙上的画中景象，

英雄、斗争和节庆；

还有那角落的玩具，

是古埃及男孩的东西。

Singing

Of **speckled** ^① eggs the birdie sings
And nests among the trees;
The sailor sings of ropes and things
In ships upon the seas.
The children sing in far Japan,
The children sing in Spain;
The **organ** ^② with the organ man
Is singing in the rain.

歌唱

① speckled ['spekld] *a.* 有斑点的

② organ ['ɔːgn] *n.* 风琴

小鸟歌唱斑斓的鸟蛋，
还有林间的鸟窝；
水手歌唱绳索和货物，
在海上的轮船里。
遥远的日本童声唱响，
西班牙的童声也嘹亮；
风琴还有那位演奏者，
正在雨中唱歌。

Looking Forward

When I am grown to man's **estate** [①]
I shall be very proud and great,
And tell the other girls and boys
Not to **meddle with** [②] my toys.

期待

① estate [i'steit] *n.* (人生的) 阶段

② meddle with 乱动

我长大成人后，
会非常强大、神气。
快快告诉其他小朋友，
千万别动我的玩偶。

A Good Play

We built a ship upon the stairs
All made of the back-bedroom chairs,
And filled it full of sofa pillows
To go a-sailing on the **billows**^①.
We took a saw and several nails,
And water in the nursery **pails**^②;
And Tom said, 'Let us also take
An apple and a slice of cake';
Which was enough for Tom and me
To go a-sailing on, till tea.
We sailed along for days and days,
And had the very best of plays;
But Tom fell out and hurt his knee,
So there was no one left but me.

好玩的游戏

① billow ['biləu] *n.* 巨浪

② pail [peil] *n.* 桶

我们在楼梯上造了艘船，
用的是卧室角落的椅子，
再用椅垫填满船舱，
准备去海上乘风破浪。
拿上一把锯条和几枚钉子，
带上提桶里的水；
汤姆说，"我们拿一个苹果
再加上一块糕饼"；
便足够我们两个出海，
到下午茶的时间再回来。
我们航行了好多好多天，
尽情尽兴地游玩；
但汤姆摔下来，磕伤了膝盖，
所以只剩我一人航海。

Where Go the Boats?

Dark brown is the river,
Golden is the sand.
It flows along for ever,
With trees on either hand.
Green leaves a-floating,
Castles of the **foam**①,
Boats of mine a-boating —
Where will all come home?
On goes the river
And out past the **mill**②,
Away down the valley,
Away down the hill.
Away down the river,
A hundred miles and more,
Other little children
Shall bring my boats **ashore**③.

小船去哪儿？

① foam [fəum] *n.* 泡沫

② mill [mil] *n.* 磨坊

③ ashore [əˈʃɔː] *ad.* 向岸

深棕色的河水，
金黄色的沙土。
河水流动不息，
树木夹岸而立。
片片绿叶轻舟，
泡沫城堡漫游，
我的那些小船，
哪里才是家园？
河水奔忙不停，
从磨坊中流出，
顺着那条山谷，
依着那座丘陵。
沿着这条河流，
一百多英里远，
会有小朋友，
带我的小船上岸。

Auntie's Skirt

Whenever Auntie moves around,
Her dresses make a **curious** [①] sound;
They **trail** [②] behind her up the floor,
And **trundle** [③] after through the door.

姑妈的裙子

① curious ['kjuəriəs] *a.* 奇
　特的
② trail [treil] *v.* 拖
③ trundle ['trʌndl] *v.* 移动

只要姑妈一转身，
裙子就会发出怪响；
上楼时裙摆拖在身后，
进门时缓缓滑过地面。

The Land of Counterpane^①

When I was sick and lay a-bed,
I had two pillows at my head,
And all my toys beside me lay
To keep me happy all day.
And sometimes for an hour or so
I watched my **leaden**^② soldiers go,
With different uniforms and **drills**^③,
Among the bed-clothes, through the hills;
And sometimes sent my ships in **fleets**^④
All up and down among the sheets;
Or brought my trees and houses out,
And planted cities all about.
I was the giant great and **still**^⑤
That sits upon the pillow-hill,
And sees before him, **dale**^⑥ and plain,
The pleasant land of counterpane.

床单大陆

① counterpane
['kauntəpein] *n.* 床罩

生病卧床的时候，

我枕着两个枕头，

玩具都摆在身边，

陪我度过快乐的一天。

② leaden ['ledn] *a.* 铅制的
③ drill [dril] *n.*（军事的）
操练
④ fleet [fli:t] *n.* 舰队

有时花一两个钟头，

看玩具士兵向前走，

穿不同的军装，做不同的动作，

在被单上，穿山越岭；

有时让船只组成队，

在床单上来来回回；

或者拿出树林和房屋，

四处建造新城都。

⑤ still [stil] *a.* 静止的，不
动的

我就是安静的巨人，

守在这枕头山丘，

⑥ dale [deil] *n.* 山谷

山谷原野，在我眼前，

这就是快乐的床单大陆。

The Land of Nod[①]

From breakfast on all through the day
At home among my friends I stay;
But every night I go abroad
Afar into the land of Nod.
All by myself I have to go,
With none to tell me what to do —
All alone beside the streams
And up the mountain-sides of dreams.
The strangest things are there for me,
Both things to eat and things to see,
And many frightening sights abroad
Till morning in the land of Nod.
Try as I like to find the way,
I never can get back by day,
Nor can remember plain and clear
The curious music that I hear.

睡梦谷

① nod [nɔd] *n.* 打盹

从早餐开始的一整天，
我和伙伴们待在家里；
可每到了晚上我都会去远方，
去那遥远的睡梦谷。
一个人上路探险，
没有人过来指点——
沿着溪流自己走，
爬上梦山的山坡。
那里的东西稀奇古怪，
吃的奇怪，看的也奇怪，
还有许多恐怖景象，
一直到睡梦谷天亮。
我虽然很喜欢探路，
但从未在白天找到归途，
听过那古怪的乐章，
也没有清晰的印象。

My Shadow

I have a little shadow that goes in and out with me,

And what can be the use of him is more than I can see.

He is very, very like me from the **heels**^① up to the head;

And I see him jump before me, when I jump into my bed.

The funniest thing about him is the way he likes to grow —

Not at all like **proper**^② children, which is always very slow;

For he sometimes shoots up taller like an **india-rubber**^③ ball,

And he sometimes gets so little that there's none of him at all.

He hasn't got a **notion**^④ of how children ought to play,

And can only **make a fool of**^⑤ me in every sort of way.

我的影子

① heel [hi:l] *n.* 脚后跟

② proper ['prɔpə] *a.* 合乎体统的

③ india-rubber [ˌindiə'rʌbə] *n.* 橡胶

④ notion ['nəuʃn] *n.* 概念

⑤ make a fool of sb. 愚弄某人

我有一个小影子，
跟着我进进出出，
要说他有什么用？
我可真是看不出。
影子和我极相像，
浑身上下全一样；
我蹦蹦跳跳上了床，
他抢先一步跳上来。
他最可笑的地方
是变起来很夸张。
一点不像规矩的小孩，
从小到大慢慢长；
他有时候像弹力球，
嗖地一下就拔高，
有时候缩得很小，
让你根本找不到。
小孩该怎么玩游戏，
他一点也没主意，
只会用各种方法，

He stays so close beside me, he's a **coward** [①] you can see;

I'd think shame to stick to nursie as that shadow sticks to me!

One morning, very early, before the sun was up,

I rose and found the shining dew on every **buttercup** [②];

But my lazy little shadow, like an **arrant** [③] sleepy-head,

Had stayed at home behind me and was fast asleep in bed.

① coward ['kauəd] n. 懦弱的人

② buttercup ['bʌtəkʌp] n. 毛茛属植物

③ arrant ['ærnt] a. 彻头彻尾的

把我耍得团团转。

他这么紧紧跟随,

明明是个胆小鬼;

我要是这样黏小保姆,

就会感到羞愧!

一天清晨,时候尚早,

太阳还没当空照,

我爬起来看到:

金凤花露珠闪耀;

而懒惰的影子,分明是个懒虫,

还在家里呼呼睡懒觉。

System

Every night my **prayers**^① I say,
And get my dinner every day;
And every day that I've been good,
I get an orange after food.
The child that is not clean and neat,
With lots of toys and things to eat,
He is a naughty child, I'm sure —
Or else his papa is **poor**^②.

规矩

① prayer [preə] *n.* 祈祷文

② poor [pɔː(r)] *a.* 差劲的

每天晚上我都祈祷，
然后领到晚餐吃好；
如果白天表现很棒，
餐后橘子便是嘉奖。
那个孩子不讲整洁，
却有很多玩的和吃的，
我敢肯定他很调皮——
要不就是他的爸爸不称职。

A Good Boy

I woke before the morning, I was happy all the day,
I never said an **ugly** [1] word, but smiled and stuck to play.
And now at last the sun is going down behind the wood,
And I am very happy, for I know that I've been good.
My bed is waiting cool and fresh, with **linen** [2] smooth and fair,
And I must off to sleepsin-by, and not forget my prayer.
I know that, till to-morrow I shall see the sun arise,
No ugly dream shall fright my mind, no ugly sight my eyes,
But **slumber** [3] hold me tightly till I waken in the dawn,
And hear the **thrushes** [4] singing in the **lilacs** [5] round the lawn.

好孩子

① ugly ['ʌgli] *a.* 道德败坏的

② linen ['linin] *n.* 亚麻织品

③ slumber ['slʌmbə] *n.* 睡眠
④ thrush [θrʌʃ] *n.* 画眉
⑤ lilac ['lailək] *n.* 丁香花

天还没亮我就起床，
从早到晚没有烦恼，
从没说出一句脏话，
微笑待人快乐玩耍。
太阳终于快要落下，
回到那片森林后边，
我的心里多么开心啊，
因为知道自己表现很好。
我的小床整洁以待，
被单也很平整可爱，
现在我该去睡觉啦，
而且不能忘记祈祷。
我知道，到明天，
太阳升起之前，
不会有惊心的噩梦，
也看不到可怕的景象，
一晚上都睡得安稳，
直到我醒来的清晨，
听到草地那边丁香丛中，
画眉在欢唱。

Escape at Bedtime

The lights from the **parlour**^① and kitchen shone out
Through the **blinds**^② and the windows and bars;
And high overhead and all moving about,
There were thousands of millions of stars.
There ne'er were such thousands of leaves on a tree,
Nor of people in church or the Park,
As the crowds of the stars that looked down upon me,
And that **glittered**^③ and **winked**^④ in the dark.
The Dog, and the Plough, and the Hunter, and all,
And the star of the sailor, and Mars,
These shone in the sky, and the pail by the wall
Would be half full of water and stars.
They saw me at last, and they chased me with cries,
And they soon had me **packed into**^⑤ bed;
But the **glory**^⑥ kept shining and bright in my eyes,
And the stars going round in my head.

睡前逃离

① parlour ['pɑːlə] n. 客厅
② blind [blaind] n. 窗帘

客厅厨房很明亮,

窗户门闩透出光;

成千上万的小星星,

在天上运转不停。

树上的叶子没这么多,

教堂或公园里的人群也比不过,

繁星点点在高处俯瞰,

③ glitter ['glitə] v. 闪光
④ wink [wiŋk] v. 闪烁

黑暗中晶晶发亮一闪一闪。

天狼星、北斗星、猎户星和火星,

还有为水手引航的星星,

挂在空中放光明,

墙边的提桶里,

装着半桶水还有星星。

⑤ pack into 塞进
⑥ glory ['glɔːri] n. 壮丽,
灿烂

终于让大人发现了我,

他们边喊边追赶,

很快把我送上床;

可是,灿烂的光芒还在眼前,

满脑子的星星不停转。

Marching Song

Bring the comb and **play upon**^① it!
Marching, here we come!
Willie **cocks**^② his **highland**^③ **bonnet**^④,
Johnnie beats the drum.
Mary Jane commands the party,
Peter leads the **rear**^⑤;
Feet in time, alert and **hearty**^⑥,
Each a **Grenadier**^⑦!
All in the most **martial**^⑧ manner
Marching double-quick;
While the napkin like a banner
Waves upon the stick!
Here's enough of fame and pillage,
Great commander Jane!
Now that we've been round the village,
Let's go home again.

进行曲

① play upon 演奏

② cock [kɔk] v. 歪戴（帽子）

③ highland ['hailənd] a.
苏格兰高地的

④ bonnet ['bɔnit] n. 软帽

⑤ rear [riə] n. 后方部队

⑥ hearty ['hɑːti] a. 精神饱
满的

⑦ Grenadier [ˌgrenə'diə]
n. 英国近卫步兵团的士
兵

⑧ martial ['mɑːʃl] a. 尚武
的

拿来梳子，开始奏乐！
齐步走，我们来啦！
威廉戴着苏格兰帽，
约翰当当把鼓敲。
玛丽·简在前率领队伍，
彼得负责压后阵；
步伐一致，庄严沉稳，
人人都是精锐士兵！
个个尽显勇武之情，
队伍加速向前行；
军旗用餐巾来充当，
在杆子上迎风飘扬！
美名远扬，战果累累，
简是英明的总司令！
围着村庄，走上一圈，
现在我们要回家啦！

The Cow

The friendly cow, all red and white,
I love **with all my heart**[①]:
She gives me cream with all her might,
To eat with apple-tart.
She wanders **lowing**[②] here and there,
And yet she cannot **stray**[③],
All in the pleasant open air,
The pleasant light of day;
And blown by all the winds that pass
And wet with all the **showers**[④],
She walks among the meadow grass
And eats the meadow flowers.

奶牛

① with all my heart 全心全意地

② low [ləu] v. 牛叫

③ stray [strei] v. 迷路，走失

④ shower ['ʃauə] n. 阵雨

友善的奶牛，皮毛红白相间，
我全心全意地喜爱：
她奉献奶油毫无保留，
让我配上苹果蛋挞好美味。
哞哞叫着到处徘徊，
最后总会乖乖回来，
辽阔的天空下尽情游荡，
明媚的日光里肆意徜徉；
任由那风吹和雨打，
她漫步在绿草中，
开心地吃着野花。

Happy Thought

The world is so full
Of **a number of**[①] things,
I'm sure we should all
Be as happy as kings.

快乐的想法

① a number of 许多

世界是如此丰富，
到处都琳琅满目，
大家应感到满足，
像国王一样幸福。

The Wind

I saw you **toss** [1] the kites on high
And blow the birds about the sky;
And all around I heard you pass,
Like ladies' skirts across the grass —
O wind, a-blowing all day long,
O wind, that sings so loud a song!
I saw the different things you did,
But always you yourself you hid.
I felt you push, I heard you call,
I could not see yourself at all —
O wind, a-blowing all day long,
O wind, that sings so loud a song!
O you that are so strong and cold,
O blower, are you young or old?
Are you a beast of field and tree,
Or just a stronger child than me?
O wind, a-blowing all day long,
O wind, that sings so loud a song!

风

① toss [tɔs] v. 投掷

你让风筝在空中飞舞，
也让鸟儿在天上翱翔；
四处都听到你的动静，
就像裙子摩挲着草坪——
风啊，整天都在吹奏，
风啊，就这样高歌一首！
你做的事情各不相同，
但总把自己隐藏其中。
你推我向前，你向我呼喊，
我却根本看不见——
风啊，整天都在吹奏，
风啊，就这样高歌一首！
你是如此的强劲寒凉，
风啊，你是年少还是年长？
你是田间树林里的野兽，
还是比我更强壮的小朋友？
风啊，整天都在吹奏，
风啊，就这样高歌一首！

Keepsake^① Mill

Over the borders, a sin without pardon,
Breaking the branches and crawling below,
Out through the breach in the wall of the garden,
Down by the banks of the river, we go.
Here is the mill with the humming of thunder,
Here is the **weir**^② with the wonder of foam,
Here is the **sluice**^③ with the race running under —
Marvellous places, though handy to home!
Sounds of the village grow stiller and stiller,
Stiller the note of the birds on the hill;
Dusty and dim are the eyes of the miller,
Deaf are his ears with the **moil**^④ of the mill.
Years may go by, and the wheel in the river
Wheel as it wheels for us, children, to-day,
Wheel and keep roaring and foaming for ever
Long after all of the boys are away.
Home from the Indies, and home from the ocean,
Heroes and soldiers we all shall come home;
Still we shall find the old mill-wheel **in motion**^⑤,

磨坊纪念品

① keepsake ['ki:pseik] *n.* 纪念品

② weir [wiə] *n.* 坝
③ sluice [slu:s] *n.* 水闸

④ moil [mɔil] *n.* 喧闹

⑤ in motion 在开动中，在运转中

越过边界，罪不可恕，
折断树枝又向前匍匐，
从院墙的裂缝中钻出，
沿着河岸，我们上路。
磨坊里机器轰鸣如雷，
河坝上涌起层层泡沫，
水闸下激流迸发——
绝妙的地方近在咫尺！
村庄里渐渐归于平静，
山上的鸟也不再争鸣；
磨坊主的双眸暗淡无光，
轰鸣声让他听不见别的声响。
一年年地过去，河里的水车，
还像今天这般咕噜咕噜地转，
喧腾的巨响从未间断，
翻滚的水花直到永远，
男孩们早已经去了远方。
不论是在印度群岛，
还是在大海上，

Turning and **churning**^① that river to foam.

You with the bean that I gave when we quarrelled,

I with your **marble**^② of Saturday last,

Honoured and old and all **gaily**^③ **apparelled**^④,

Here we shall meet and remember the past.

① churn [tʃəːn] v. 搅动

② marble ['mɑːbl] n. 弹珠
③ gaily ['geili] ad. 华丽地
④ apparel [ə'pærl] v.
　　给……穿衣

英雄和士兵都将回家；
破旧的水车依然在那里旋转，
翻腾的河水泡沫不断。
你拿着我们吵架时我给你的蚕豆，
我拿着上周六你给我的玻璃球，
凯旋归来的老人穿着漂亮衣裳，
相约在这里追忆旧时光。

Good and Bad Children

Children, you are very little,
And your bones are very **brittle**①;
If you would grow great and **stately**②,
You must try to walk **sedately**③.
You must still be bright and quiet,
And **content with**④ simple diet;
And remain, through all **bewild'ring**⑤,
Innocent and honest children.
Happy hearts and happy faces,
Happy play in grassy places —
That was how, in ancient ages,
Children grew to kings and **sages**⑥.
But the unkind and the **unruly**⑦,
And the sort to eat **unduly**⑧,
They must never hope for glory —
Theirs is quite a different story!
Cruel children, crying babies,
All grow up as **geese**⑨ and **gabies**⑩,
Hated, as their age increases,
By their nephews and their nieces.

好孩子和坏孩子

① brittle ['britl] *a.* 脆弱的
② stately ['steitli] *a.* 器宇不凡的
③ sedately [si'detli] *ad.* 沉着地
④ be content with 满足的
⑤ bewildering [bi'wildriŋ] *a.* 使人困惑的

⑥ sage [seidʒ] *n.* 贤者
⑦ unruly [ʌn'ru:li] *a.* 任性的
⑧ unduly [ʌn'dju:li] *ad.* 过度地

⑨ geese [gi:s] *n.*（goose 的复数形式）傻瓜
⑩ gaby [geibi] *n.* 傻瓜

孩子们，你们还很小，
骨骼还没有长好；
要想长大气度不凡，
就要踏实走路多锻炼。
聪明安分很重要，
粗茶淡饭也逍遥；
就算各种困惑在眼前，
天真诚实是底线。
心情愉快多欢笑，
草上游戏乐陶陶，
古代的孩子就这样，
变成了君王和圣贤。
可是有些孩子任性不友善，
贪吃贪喝不听话，
他们一生不会有辉煌，
步入歧途真可怕！
不讲道理，哭哭啼啼，
长大后都不会如意，
岁数一天一天往上长，
侄儿侄女看他们都嫌烦。

Foreign Children

Little Indian, **Sioux**^① or **Crow**^②,
Little frosty Eskimo,
Little Turk or Japanee,
O! don't you wish that you were me?
You have seen the **scarlet**^③ trees
And the lions over seas;
You have eaten **ostrich**^④ eggs,
And turned the turtles off their legs.
Such a life is very fine,
But it's not so nice as mine;
You must often, as you **trod**^⑤,
Have wearied not to be abroad.
You have curious things to eat,
I am fed on proper meat;
You must dwell beyond the foam,
But I am safe and live at home.
Little Indian, Sioux or Crow,
Little frosty Eskimo,
Little Turk or Japanee,
O! don't you wish that you were me?

外国的小孩

① Sioux [su:] *n.* 苏人（印第安人的一支）
② Crow [krəu] *n.* 克劳人（印第安人的一支）

③ scarlet ['skɑ:lət] *a.* 深红色的

④ ostrich ['ɔstritʃ] *n.* 鸵鸟

⑤ trod [trɔd] *v.*（tread 的过去式）行走

印第安的苏族、克劳族小朋友，
冰天雪地里的爱斯基摩小朋友，
土耳其小朋友，日本小朋友，
哦，你们是否希望和我一样？
你们见过红色的树木，
还曾见过海外的雄狮；
你们吃过鸵鸟的蛋，
连海龟也是盘中餐。
这样的生活好是好，
可和我相比还是不如我；
你们奔波时，肯定常厌倦，
不想总是跑得很远。
你们吃的是奇怪的东西，
我吃的是像样的肉食；
你们在外漂泊流浪，
我在家里安然无恙。
印第安的苏族、克劳族小朋友，
冰天雪地里的爱斯基摩小朋友，
土耳其小朋友，日本小朋友，
哦，你们是否希望和我一样？

The Sun's Travels

The sun is not a-bed when I
At night upon my pillow lie;
Still round the earth his way he takes,
And morning after morning makes.
While here at home, in shining day,
We round the sunny garden play,
Each little Indian sleepy-head
Is being kissed and put to bed.
And when at eve I rise from tea,
Day dawns beyond the Atlantic Sea,
And all the children in the West
Are getting up and being dressed.

太阳的旅行

晚上我要躺下休息，
太阳还在忙个不停；
仍然绕着地球旋转，
每天早上都来相见。
我们家这里阳光灿烂，
我们绕着那花园玩，
印度小孩睡眼蒙眬，
亲亲脸颊上床入眠。
傍晚我吃完茶点起身，
大西洋对岸已是清晨，
西方的所有小朋友，
都在准备起床穿衣裳。

The Lamplighter[①]

My tea is nearly ready
And the sun has left the sky;
It's time to take the window
To see Leerie going by;
For every night at tea-time
And before you take your seat,
With **lantern**[②] and with ladder
He comes posting up the street.
Now Tom would be a driver
And Maria go to sea,
And my papa's a **banker**[③]
And as rich as he can be;
But I, when I am stronger
And can choose what I'm to do,
O Leerie, I'll **go round**[④] at night
And light the lamps with you!
For we are very lucky,
With a lamp before the door,
And Leerie stops to light it

灯夫

① lamplighter ['læmplaitə]
n. 点燃街灯的灯夫

我的茶点就快准备好,

太阳不再当空照;

是时候守在窗边了,

看着李尔从窗前经过;

每到傍晚茶点时间,

② lantern ['læntən] n. 灯笼

在你还没就座之前,

李尔拿着灯笼和梯子,

在街上把灯挂起。

汤姆想成为驾驶员,

玛利亚要出海探险,

③ banker ['bæŋkə] n. 银行
家

我爸爸是位银行家,

努力赚钱不甘落下;

可我却想,等到长得更强壮,

自己选择我想做的行当,

④ go round 到处走动

李尔,我想和你一起晚上出去

把路上的一盏盏灯点亮!

我们的运气多么好,

门前就有一盏灯,

李尔停下点亮它,

As he lights so many more;
And O! before you hurry by
With ladder and with light,
O Leerie, see a little child
And nod to him to-night!

他还让更多路灯有了光芒；
哦！李尔，
今晚你拿着
梯子和灯笼匆匆过，
要是看到一个小朋友，
请你一定向他点点头。

My Bed Is a Boat

My bed is like a little boat;
Nurse helps me when I **embark** ① ;
She **girds** ② me in my sailor's coat
And **starts** ③ me in the dark.
At night, I go on board and say
Good-night to all my friends on shore;
I shut my eyes and sail away
And see and hear no more.
And sometimes things to bed I take,
As **prudent** ④ sailors have to do;
Perhaps a slice of wedding-cake,
Perhaps a toy or two.
All night across the dark we steer:
But when the day returns at last,
Safe in my room, beside the **pier** ⑤ ,
I find my vessel **fast** ⑥ .

我的床是条船

① embark [im'bɑ:k] v. 上船
② gird [gə:d] v. 用腰带束衣服
③ start [stɑ:t] v. 使开始

④ prudent ['pru:dnt] a. 谨慎的

⑤ pier [piə] n. 码头
⑥ fast [fɑ:st] ad. 牢固地

我的小床像船一样；
上船时保姆来帮忙；
她为我穿好水手服，
漆黑夜里送我上路。
晚上，我登上小船，
祝岸上的朋友们晚安；
我合上眼睛出海远行，
寂静无声不见一个人影。
我学那严谨的海员：
有时备些东西放在身边，
也许是一块婚礼上的蛋糕，
也许带一两个玩具也很好。
整整一夜我们在黑暗中航行：
终于等到天空重新变亮，
只见小船驶入海港，
在房间里安然无恙。

The Moon

The moon has a face like the clock in the hall;
She shines on thieves on the garden wall,
On streets and fields and harbor **quays** [1] ,
And birdies asleep in the forks of the trees.
The **squalling** [2] cat and the **squeaking** [3] mouse,
The **howling** [4] dog by the door of the house,
The bat that lies in bed at noon,
All love to be out by the light of the moon.
But all of the things that belong to the day
Cuddle [5] to sleep to be out of her way;
And flowers and children close their eyes
Till up in the morning the sun shall rise.

月亮

① quay [kiː] *n.* 码头

② squall ['skwɔːl] *v.* 尖叫

③ squeak [skwiːk] *v.* 吱吱叫

④ howling ['haulɪŋ] *a.* 咆哮的

⑤ cuddle ['kʌdl] *v.* 依偎

月亮那圆圆的脸庞，
像门厅里的钟表一样，
她照亮花园围墙上的小偷，
照亮马路、田野和港口，
照亮树枝上酣睡的小鸟。
喵喵叫的猫和吱吱叫的鼠，
房屋门口吠叫的狗，
还有中午才睡觉的蝙蝠，
全都喜欢在月光下登场。
那些属于白天的生灵，
此刻都已在一边相拥睡觉；
花朵和小孩都合上眼，
等到早晨太阳升上天。

The Swing

How do you like to go up in a swing,
Up in the air so blue?
Oh, I do think it the pleasantest thing
Ever a child can do!

Up in the air and over the wall,
Till I can see so wide,
Rivers and trees and cattle and all
Over the countryside —

Till I look down on the garden green,
Down on the roof so brown —
Up in the air I go flying again,
Up in the air and down!

秋千

想不想去荡秋千，
高高飞到天空上。
哦，对于我们小朋友，
这真是最大的享受！
飞到空中比墙高，
视野开阔风光好，
河流树林和牛群，
村庄处处是美景。
青青园地在眼中，
还有屋顶褐色浓——
高高飞在天空里，
飞上空中再下落！

Time to Rise

A birdie with a yellow **bill** [1]
Hopped upon the window **sill** [2].
Cocked his shining **eye** [3] and said:
'Ain't you 'shamed, you sleepy-head?'

该起床了

① bill [bil] *n.* 喙
② sill [sil] *n.* 窗台
③ cock an eye 凝神细看

黄色喙的小鸟好轻盈，
在窗台上跳个不停。
明亮的眼睛看着我，叫道：
"小瞌睡虫，害不害羞？"

Looking-Glass River

Smooth it slides upon its travel,

Here a **wimple** [①], there a **gleam** [②] —

O the clean **gravel** [③]!

O the smooth stream!

Sailing blossoms, silver fishes,

Paven [④] pools as clear as air —

How a child wishes

To live down there!

We can see our colored faces

Floating on the shaken pool

Down in the cool places,

Dim and very cool;

Till a wind or water wrinkle,

Dipping [⑤] **marten** [⑥], **plumping** [⑦] **trout** [⑧],

Spreads in a twinkle

And **blots** all **out** [⑨].

See the rings pursue each other;

All below grows black as night,

Just as if mother

镜子河

① wimple ['wimpl] *n.* 涟漪
② gleam [gli:m] *n.* 闪光
③ gravel ['grævl] *n.* 碎石

④ paven [peivn] *a.*（同 paved）用石头铺的

⑤ dip [dip] *v.* 下沉
⑥ marten ['mɑ:tin] *n.* 貂
⑦ plump [plʌmp] *v.* 坠下
⑧ trout [traut] *n.* 鲑鱼
⑨ blot out 遮掉

小河静静地流淌，
这里有水花，那里在闪烁——
哦，干净的石头！
哦，平静的小溪流！
花瓣漂下，银鱼成群，
水池就像空气一样透亮，
小朋友多么希望
从此以后就住在这里！
我们粉扑扑的脸庞
荡漾在水波上，
在那些阴凉的地方，
光线暗淡非常清凉；
风吹浪起的时候，
水貂下潜，鲑鱼沉水，
闪闪发亮的波纹，
把一切遮掉。
扩散的水圈你追我赶；
水的下面像黑沉沉的夜晚，
这就好像

Had blown out of light!
Patience, children, just a minute —
See the spreading circles **die**[①];
The stream and all in it
Will clear by-and-by.

① die [dai] v. 消失

妈妈把灯烛吹灭！

耐心点，孩子们，马上就好，

那水圈纷纷跑掉；

小溪还有里面的一切，

又会回到往昔的清冽。

Fairy Bread^①

Come up here, O dusty feet!
Here is fairy bread to eat.
Here in my retiring room,
Children, you may **dine**
On^② the golden smell of **broom**^③
And the shade of pine;
And when you have eaten well,
Fairy stories hear and tell.

仙女面包

① fairy bread 仙女面包，
彩糖面包（涂有黄油，
撒有小彩糖的面包片）

② dine on 吃……
③ broom [bru:m] *n.* 金雀花

快来，风尘仆仆的小孩！
仙女面包已备好。
这是我的休息室，
小朋友们，请用餐，
有金雀花送来芬芳，
有松树为我们遮阳；
等你们吃好饭，
就可以讲故事玩。

From a Railway Carriage

Faster than fairies, faster than witches,
Bridges and houses, **hedges**[1] and **ditches**[2];
And charging along like troops in a battle,
All through the meadows the horses and cattle:
All of the sights of the hill and the plain
Fly as thick as **driving rain**[3];
And ever again, in the wink of an eye,
Painted stations whistle by.
Here is a child who **clambers**[4] and **scrambles**[5],
All by himself and gathering **brambles**[6];
Here is a **tramp**[7] who stands and gazes;
And there is the green for stringing the daisies!
Here is a **cart**[8] run away in the road
Lumping[9] along with the man and load;
And here is a mill, and there is a river:
Each a **glimpse**[10] and gone for ever!

在火车车厢上

① hedge [hedʒ] *n.* 树篱
② ditch [ditʃ] *n.* 沟渠

③ driving rain 倾盆大雨

④ clamber ['klæmbə] *v.* 爬上
⑤ scramble ['skræmbl] *v.* 爬行
⑥ bramble ['bræmbl] *n.* 黑莓
⑦ tramp [træmp] *n.* 流浪者
⑧ cart [kɑːt] *n.* 二轮运货马车
⑨ lump [lʌmp] *v.* 笨重地移动
⑩ glimpse [glim(p)s] *n.* 一瞥

比精灵还快，比女巫还快，
桥路房屋，篱笆水渠；
像部队打仗冲向前方，
马匹和牛群遍布草场：
目光所及的山川大地，
像骤雨那样迅疾浓密；
眨眼工夫，又是一站，
汽笛声中驶过向前。
有个小朋友爬得很辛苦，
一个人在采野莓；
有个流浪汉站着凝望；
草地把雏菊串成行！
马车正在赶路，
载人拉货真不轻松；
还有磨坊，还有小河，
看了一眼便永不相见！

Winter-Time

Late lies the **wintry** ① sun a-bed,
A **frosty** ②, **fiery** ③ sleepy-head;
Blinks ④ but an hour or two; and then,
A blood-red orange, sets again.
Before the stars have left the skies,
At morning in the dark I rise;
And **shivering** ⑤ in my **nakedness** ⑥,
By the cold candle, **bathe** ⑦ and dress.
Close by the jolly fire I sit
To warm my frozen bones a bit;
Or with a **reindeer-sled** ⑧, explore
The colder countries round the door.
When, to go out, my nurse **doth** ⑨ wrap
Me in my **comforter** ⑩ and cap:
The cold wind burns my face, and blows
Its frosty pepper up my nose.
Black are my steps on silver **sod** ⑪;
Thick blows my frosty breath abroad;
And tree and house, and hill and lake,
Are frosted like a wedding-cake.

冬日时光

① wintry [wintri] *a.* 冬天的
② frosty ['frɔsti] *a.* 灰白的
③ fiery ['faiəri] *a.* 火焰的
④ blink [bliŋk] *v.* 闪烁

⑤ shiver ['ʃivə] *v.* 颤抖
⑥ nakedness ['neikidnis]
　　n. 赤裸
⑦ bathe [beið] *v.* 洗澡

⑧ reindeer-sled
　　['reindiə'sled] *n.* 驯鹿雪
　　橇
⑨ doth [dʌθ] *v.* 〈古〉do
　　的第三人称单数现在式
⑩ comforter ['kʌmfətə] *n.*
　　〈旧〉羊毛围巾

⑪ sod [sɔd] *n.* 草地

冬天太阳很晚起床，
懒惰的火球结白霜；
忽闪忽闪个把钟头，
一轮红日就把工收。
天上星星还没退场，
天还黑着我就起床；
光着身子瑟瑟发抖，
冷烛照我洗澡穿衣。
赶快坐在炉火旁边，
暖暖身子舒展一点；
或者坐上驯鹿雪橇，
到门口的寒地去寻宝。
出门时，总少不了
围巾帽子把我包好：
寒风嗖嗖地刮过脸庞，
吹起雪花落在鼻子上。
银白的地上踩下黑色的脚印；
哈出一大团的白雾；
树木房屋，山川湖泊，
银装素裹像婚礼上的白色蛋糕。

The Hayloft[①]

Through all the pleasant meadow-side
The grass grew shoulder-high,
Till the shining **scythes**[②] went far and wide
And cut it down to dry.
These green and sweetly smelling drops
They led in **wagons**[③] home;
And they piled them here in mountain tops
For mountaineers to roam.
Here is Mount Clear, Mount **Rusty**[④]-Nail,
Mount Eagle and Mount High; —
The mice that in these mountains dwell,
No happier are than I!
O what a joy to clamber there,
O what a place for play,
With the sweet, the dim, the dusty air,
The happy hills of hay.

干草棚

① hayloft ['heilɔft] *n.* 干草棚

② scythe [saið] *n.* 长柄大镰刀

③ wagon ['wægn] *n.* 货车

④ rusty ['rʌsti] *a.* 生锈的

美丽的原野处处笼罩，
草儿长得与肩同高，
银刀闪闪穿梭其间，
割下青草去晒干。
割下的草翠绿清香，
他们用货车拉回家；
青草堆成一座座小山，
登山的人们前来游览。
晴朗峰，锈钉山，
还有鹰山和高山——
山中住着小老鼠，
都没有我快乐！
哦，多么喜欢爬山，
哦，这里多么好玩，
清香，幽暗，扬起灰，
这就是快快乐乐的干草堆。

Farewell to the Farm

The **coach**① is at the door at last;
The eager children, **mounting**② fast
And kissing hands, **in chorus**③ sing:
Good-bye, good-bye, to everything!
To house and garden, field and lawn,
The meadow-gates we swang upon,
To **pump**④ and **stable**⑤, tree and swing,
Good-bye, good-bye, to everything!
And fare you well **for evermore**⑥,
O ladder at the hayloft door,
O hayloft where the **cobwebs**⑦ **cling**⑧,
Good-bye, good-bye, to everything!
Crack goes the **whip**⑨, and off we go;
The trees and houses smaller grow;
Last, round the woody turn we **swing**⑩:
Good-bye, good-bye, to everything!

告别农场

① coach [kəutʃ] *n.* 四轮大马车
② mount [maunt] *v.* 爬上
③ in chorus 一齐

④ pump [pʌmp] *n.* 水泵
⑤ stable ['steibl] *n.* 牛棚

⑥ for evermore 永远

⑦ cobweb ['kɔbweb] *n.* 蜘蛛网
⑧ cling [kliŋ] *v.* 附着

⑨ whip [wip] *n.* 鞭子

⑩ swing [swiŋ] *v.* 转向

马车终于来到门前；
小孩急着冲到里面，
挥手飞吻，一起唱道：
再见了，再见，所有的一切！
房子花园，田野草坪，
被我们摇来晃去的牧场大门，
水泵牛棚，树木秋千，
再见了，再见，所有的一切！
从此我们不再相见，
哦，干草棚门口的爬梯，
哦，干草棚里蜘蛛网布，
再见了，再见，所有的一切！
清脆的一鞭，我们上路；
树木和房屋变得越来越小；
终于，我们在树林那里转弯：
再见了，再见，所有的一切！

North-West Passage

1. Good night

When the bright lamp is carried in,
The sunless hours again begin;
O'er all without, in field and lane,
The **haunted**[1] night returns again.
Now we **behold**[2] the **embers**[3] **flee**[4]
About the firelit **hearth**[5]; and see
Our faces painted as we pass,
Like pictures, on the window-glass.
Must we to bed indeed? Well then,
Let us arise and go like men,
And face with an **undaunted**[6] **tread**[7]
The long black passage up to bed.
Farewell, O brother, sister, **sire**[8]!
O pleasant party round the fire!
The songs you sing, the tales you tell,
Till far to-morrow, fare ye well!

西北走廊

1. 晚安

① haunted ['hɔːntid] *a.* 闹
鬼的，鬼魂出没的
② behold [bi'həuld] *v.* 看见
③ ember ['embə] *n.* 灰烬
④ flee [fliː] *v.* 消散
⑤ hearth [hɑːθ] *n.* 壁炉地
面

⑥ undaunted [ʌn'dɔːntid] *a.*
勇敢的，无畏的
⑦ tread [tred] *n.* 步态

⑧ sire [saiə] *n.* 父亲

灯烛拿到屋里面，
又是日落的时间；
每一处田间小路，
再次降临鬼魂游荡夜幕。
眼前有炉灰飞舞，
绕着点火的壁炉；
玻璃窗上，像挂画，
是我们走过时映红的脸颊，
一定要去睡觉了吗？好吧，
像大人一样站起来离开，
面对去睡觉的暗暗长路，
迈出坚定有力的脚步。
明天见，哥哥姐姐和父亲！
围炉的欢聚多么陶醉！
你们唱歌，你们叙谈，
等到明天，我们再见！

2. *Shadow March*

All round the house is the jet-black night;
It stares through the **window-pane**①;
It crawls in the corners, **hiding from**② the light,
And it moves with the moving flame.
Now my little heart goes a-beating like a drum,
With the breath of the **Bogie**③ in my hair;
And all round the candle the **crooked**④ shadows come
And go marching along up the stair.
The shadows of the **balusters**⑤, the shadow of the lamp,
The shadow of the child that goes to bed —
All the wicked shadows coming, tramp, tramp, tramp,
With the black light overhead.

3. *In Port*

Last, to the chamber where I lie
My fearful footsteps **patter**⑥ **nigh**⑦,
And come from out the cold and gloom
Into my warm and cheerful room.
There, safe arrived, we turn about
To keep the coming shadows out,
And close the happy door at last
On all the **perils**⑧ that we past.
Then, when mamma goes by to bed,
She shall come in with tip-toed tread,
And see me lying warm and fast
And in the Land of Nod at last.

2. 影子的行进

黑夜把房子通通包围，
从窗外紧紧盯着屋内；
爬到角落，躲着光，
跟着火焰摇摇晃晃。
我心里像打鼓咚咚直跳，
头发里有幽灵报到；
阴影从四周向蜡烛涌来，
沿着楼梯上了高处。
栏杆的影子，灯的影子
小孩回去的影子，
咚，咚，咚，
黑暗的烛光在天花板上，
可怖的影子全都到场。

3. 出港

终于，朝着我的卧房，
胆怯的脚步连连作响，
从那寒冷阴暗的外面，
回到温馨可爱的房间。
抵达后，转过身来，
把跟着的阴影都赶出门外，
幸福的门终于合上，
途中的险恶纷纷退场。
妈妈睡前过来看看，
进来会踮着脚尖，
看我睡得安稳没有着凉，
终于抵达了睡梦谷。

① window-pane
['windəu'pein] *n.* 窗玻璃
② hide from 躲藏

③ bogy ['bəugi] *n.* 妖怪
④ crooked ['krukid] *a.* 弯曲的

⑤ baluster ['bæləstə] *n.* 栏杆

⑥ patter ['pætə] *v.* 发出急速轻拍声
⑦ nigh [nai] *ad.* 在附近地

⑧ peril ['peril] *n.* 危险

The Child Alone

独自一人

The Unseen Playmate

When children are playing alone on the green,
In comes the playmate that never was seen.
When children are happy and lonely and good,
The Friend of the Children comes out of the wood.
Nobody heard him and nobody saw,
His is a picture you never could draw,
But he's sure to be present, abroad or at home,
When children are happy and playing alone.
He lies in the **laurels** ①, he runs on the grass,
He sings when you **tinkle** ② the musical glass;
Whene'er you are happy and cannot tell why,
The Friend of the Children is sure to be by!
He loves to be little, he hates to be big,
'Tis he that inhabits the caves that you dig;
'Tis he when you play with your soldiers of **tin** ③
That sides with the Frenchmen and never can win.
'Tis he, when at night you **go off to** ④ your bed,
Bids ⑤ you go to your sleep and not trouble your head;
For wherever they're lying, in cupboard or shelf,
'Tis he will take care of your playthings himself!

新伙伴

① laurel ['lɔrl] *n.* 月桂树
② tinkle ['tiŋkl] *v.* 使发清脆的响声

③ tin [tin] *n.* 锡

④ go off to 动身前往
⑤ bid [bid] *v.* 吩咐

小朋友们在草地上自己玩，
来了一位没见过的伙伴。
小朋友们开心听话的时候，
森林中就出现这位朋友。
没人听说也没人见过，
他的样子你不可能描摹，
只要小朋友们自己好好玩耍，
他一定出现，无论在哪。
月桂丛中休息，草地上奔忙，
用玻璃杯奏乐他会歌唱；
不论为何只要你感到快乐，
这位朋友准会出现在这！
他喜欢小巧身型，
可不喜欢变得高大，
你挖的洞是他的栖息地；
你和玩具士兵们玩游戏，
他和法军一边总吃败仗。
晚上你要去睡觉的时候，
他让你好好休息别发愁；
无论玩具落在哪，餐橱里或柜子上，
他会亲自收拾帮你忙！

My Ship and I

O it's I that am the **captain**^{①} of a tidy little ship,

Of a ship that goes a-sailing on the pond;

And my ship it keeps a-turning all around and all about;

But when I'm a little older, I shall find the secret out

How to send my vessel sailing on beyond.

For I mean to grow as little as the dolly at the **helm**^{②},

And the dolly I intend to **come alive**^{③};

And with him beside to help me, it's a-sailing I shall go,

It's a-sailing on the water, when the jolly breezes blow

And the vessel goes a divie-divie dive.

O it's then you'll see me sailing through the **rushes**^{④} and the **reeds**^{⑤},

And you'll hear the water singing at the **prow**^{⑥};

For beside the dolly sailor, I'm to voyage and explore,

To land upon the island where no dolly was before,

And to fire the penny **cannon**^{⑦} in the **bow**^{⑧}.

我和我的船

① captain ['kæptin] *n.* 船长

② helm [helm] *n.* 舵
③ come alive 活跃起来

④ rush [rʌʃ] *n.* 灯芯草
⑤ reed [ri:d] *n.* 芦苇
⑥ prow [prau] *n.* 船头

⑦ cannon ['kænən] *n.* 大炮
⑧ bow [bau] *n.* 船头

一艘小船在池塘上，
小船整洁我是船长；
小船总是到处打转；
等我岁数变大，会发现，
如何让船行得更远。
我要变成舵轮的玩具娃娃那么大，
还要让娃娃开口说话；
有他在身边帮忙，我们要去远航。
在水上，微风很舒畅。
小船忽上忽下颠簸不停。
又在激流与芦苇中穿行，
船头的水流声欢快好听；
娃娃水手在身边，我要起航去探险，
在没人的小岛上岸，
把船头一便士买来的大炮点燃。

My Kingdom

Down by a shining water **well** [1]
I found a very little **dell** [2],
No higher than my head.
The **heather** [3] and the **gorse** [4] about
In summer bloom were coming out,
Some yellow and some red.
I called the little pool a sea;
The little hills were big to me;
For I am very small.
I made a boat, I made a town,
I searched the **caverns** [5] up and down,
And named them one and all.
And all about was mine, I said,
The little **sparrows** [6] overhead,
The little **minnows** [7] too.
This was the world and I was king;
For me the bees came by to sing,
For me the **swallows** [8] flew.
I played there were no deeper seas,

我的王国

① well [wel] *n.* 源泉
② dell [del] *n.* 有树林的小
谷地

③ heather ['heðə] *n.* 石楠
④ gorse [gɔ:s] *n.* 金雀花

晶晶亮的水泉边，
我找到一个小山谷，
和我长得一般高。
石楠花和金雀花，
夏日里花繁叶茂，
有黄花也有红花。
我把池塘当海洋，
我看小山都那么高；
因为我还很小。

⑤ cavern ['kævn] *n.* 洞穴

造了小船，建好城镇，
爬上爬下去找山洞，
还给他们都起好名字。
这一切都属于我，

⑥ sparrow ['spærəu] *n.* 麻
雀
⑦ minnow ['minəu] *n.* 鲦鱼

天上的小麻雀，
水里的小银鱼。
这是世界，我是君王；
蜜蜂为我来歌唱，

⑧ swallow ['swɔləu] *n.* 燕
子

燕子也为我飞来。
从没见过这么深的海，

Nor any wider plains than these,
No other kings than me.
At last I heard my mother call
Out from the house at **even-fall** [1] ,
To call me home to tea.
And I must rise and leave my dell,
And leave my dimpled water well,
And leave my heather blooms.
Alas! And as my home I neared,
How very big my nurse appeared,
How great and cool the rooms!

① even-fall ['i:vən'fɔ:l] *n.*
黄昏

没见过这么宽广的原野，
在这里我独自称王。
终于听到妈妈的呼唤，
傍晚从家里传来，
让我回去吃茶点。
起身离开小山谷，
离开叮咚的水泉，
离开石楠花。
哎！回家的路上，
保姆的身影多么高大，
多么宽敞而冰凉的房间！

Picture-Books in Winter

Summer fading, winter comes —
Frosty mornings, **tingling**^① thumbs,
Window **robins**^②, winter **rooks**^③,
And the picture story-books.

Water now is turned to stone
Nurse and I can walk upon;
Still we find the flowing **brooks**^④
In the picture story-books.

All the pretty things put by,
Wait upon the children's eye,
Sheep and shepherds, trees and **crooks**^⑤,
In the picture story-books.

We may see how all things are,
Seas and cities, near and far,
And the flying fairies' looks,
In the picture story-books.

How am I to sing your praise,
Happy chimney-corner days,
Sitting safe in nursery **nooks**^⑥,
Reading picture story-books?

冬天的图画书

① tingle ['tiŋgl] *v.* 刺痛
② robin ['rɔbin] *n.* 知更鸟
③ rook [ruk] *n.* 白嘴鸦

④ brook [bruk] *n.* 小溪

⑤ crook [kruk] *n.*（牧羊人的）曲柄杖

⑥ nook [nuk] *n.* 角落

夏天走远，冬天登场——
冰凉的早晨，手指都冻僵，
知更鸟在窗边，乌鸦会出现，
还有图画故事书。
河水冻得硬如石头，
保姆和我在上面走；
可在图画故事书里，
仍然有潺潺的溪流。
美丽的事物都画好，
孩子的眼睛会找到，
羊群和牧童，树林和牧童的曲柄杖，
图画故事书里全都有。
我们看见世界万物，
海洋和城市，不论远或近，
还有飞舞的精灵，
全都出现在图画故事书里。
我该怎样赞美你啊，
快乐的炉边时光，
孩子在儿童室角落里坐坐好，
看图画故事书多美妙？

My Treasures

These nuts that I keep in the back of the nest
Where all my **lead**^① soldiers are lying at rest,
Were gathered in autumn by nursie and me
In a wood with a well by the side of the sea.
This whistle we made (and how clearly it sounds!)
By the side of a field at the end of the grounds.
Of a branch of a **plane**^②, with a knife of my own,
It was nursie who made it, and nursie alone!
The stone, with the white and the yellow and grey,
We discovered I cannot tell how far away;
And I carried it back although weary and cold,
For though father denies it, I'm sure it is gold.
But of all my treasures the last is the king,
For there's very few children possess such a thing;
And that is a **chisel**^③, both handle and blade,
Which a man who was really a **carpenter**^④ made.

我的宝物

① lead [liːd] *n.* 铅

② plane [plein] *n.* 悬铃木

③ chisel ['tʃɪzl] *n.* 凿子
④ carpenter [kɑːpəntə(r)] *n.*
　　木匠

干果放在鸟巢里面，

玩具士兵全都躺在那边，

海边有水泉的树林里，

保姆和我秋天去采集。

我们做的口哨多么响亮！

就在尽头的田野边上。

用悬铃木枝和我的小刀，

这都是保姆一人的功劳！

那个三色石块，白、黄和灰色，

不知走了多远，我们才找到；

又累又冷我还是带回家，

那可是金子做的，虽然爸爸不这么认为。

最后一件宝贝最厉害，

是对孩子少有的优待，

一把凿子，有刀柄刀片，

这是地道木匠做的物件。

Block① City

What are you able to build with your blocks?
Castle and palaces, temples and **docks**②.
Rain may keep raining, and others go roam,
But I can be happy and building at home.
Let the sofa be mountains, the carpet be sea,
There I'll establish a city for me:
A **kirk**③ and a mill and a palace beside,
And a harbor as well where my vessels may ride.
Great is the palace with pillar and wall,
A sort of a tower on the top of it all,
And steps coming down in an **orderly**④ way
To where my toy vessels lie safe in the bay.
This one is sailing and that one is **moored**⑤:
Hark⑥ to the song of the sailors on board!
And see on the steps of my palace, the kings
Coming and going with presents and things!
Now I have done with it, down let it go!
All in a moment the town is laid low.
Block upon block lying **scattered**⑦ and free,

积木城

① block [blɔk] n. 积木
② dock [dɔk] n. 码头

③ kirk [kə:k] n. 教堂

④ orderly ['ɔ:dli] a. 整齐的

⑤ moor [mɔ:] v. 使停泊
⑥ hark [hɑ:k] v. 听（常用于命令句）

⑦ scattered ['skætəd] a. 分散的

你怎样用积木盖楼？

城堡和宫殿，寺庙和码头。

也许阴雨不散，行人不断，

而我很乐意在家里搭建。

软椅是山，地毯是海，

我的城市在这里开创：

教堂磨坊宫殿在一边，

港口用来靠岸或登船。

大宫殿里有柱子围墙，

有一个尖塔在房顶上，

规整的台阶向下伸展，

直达停玩具船的港湾。

这艘出海，那艘入港，

听，船上的水手歌声洪亮！

看，各国君王踏着宫殿的台阶，

带着礼物来来往往！

现在完工，可以拆除！

城镇一瞬间变了模样。

一堆堆积木散得到处都是，

What is there left of my town by the sea?
Yet as I saw it, I see it again;
The kirk and the palace, the ships and the men,
And as long as I live, and where'er I may be,
I'll always remember my town by the sea.

海边的城市还剩什么？
我又看见城市的样子：
教堂和宫殿，船只和海员，
无论在哪，我的生命里，
总有那座海边城市的记忆。

The Land of Story-Books

At evening when the lamp is lit,
Around the fire my parents sit;
They sit at home and talk and sing,
And do not play at anything.
Now, with my little gun, I crawl
All in the dark along the wall,
And follow round the forest track
Away behind the sofa back.
There, in the night, where none can **spy**[①],
All in my hunter's camp I lie,
And play at books that I have read
Till it is time to go to bed.
These are the hills, these are the woods,
These are my starry **solitudes**[②];
And there the river by whose brink
The roaring lions come to drink.
I see the others far away
As if in firelit camp they lay,
And I, like to an Indian **scout**[③],

故事书王国

晚上点亮灯的时候，
大人们坐在炉火左右，
坐在家里聊天唱歌，
什么游戏都不玩乐。
我带上小枪，匍匐向前，
黑暗之中沿着墙边，
顺着森林的小路，
躲到软椅的后面。

① spy [spai] *v.* 发现

晚上，那里无人看见，
自己躺在狩猎营帐，
按书里讲的玩一玩，
能够玩到睡觉前。

② solitude ['sɔlitjuːd] *n.* 荒僻的地方

这是山丘，那是树木，
这是繁星下的秘密基地；
还有那条河水边，
咆哮的狮子来饮泉。
我看见远处的人们，
似乎躺在亮灯的帐篷里，

③ scout [skaut] *n.* 侦察兵

而我，像个印第安侦察兵，

Around their party **prowled** ^① about.
So, when my nurse comes in for me,
Home I return across the sea,
And go to bed with backward books
At my dear land of Story-books.

① prowl [praul] *v.* 潜行

绕着他们去找吃的东西。
保姆来找我的时候，
跨海返回到家里头。
睡觉时有书本陪我，
有心爱的故事书王国。

Armies in the Fire

The lamps now glitter down the street;
Faintly sound the falling feet;
And the blue even slowly falls
About the garden trees and walls.
Now in the falling of the gloom
The red fire paints the empty room:
And warmly on the roof it looks,
And **flickers** [1] on the backs of books.
Armies march by tower and spire
Of cities **blazing** [2], in the fire;
Till as I gaze with staring eyes,
The armies fade, the **lustre** [3] dies.
Then once again the glow returns;
Again the **phantom** [4] city burns;
And down the red-hot valley, lo!
The phantom armies marching go!
Blinking embers, tell me true,
Where are those armies marching to,
And what the burning city is
That **crumbles** [5] in your **furnaces** [6]!

火中的军队

街上路灯闪着光亮，
几乎听不到脚步声响；
蓝色夜幕缓缓下降，
笼罩花园里的树木和围墙。
现在黑压压的一片，
火焰映红空空的房间，
暖洋洋地向着屋顶，
照得书脊上亮光闪闪。
火中城市宝塔耸立，
行进的军队经过此地；
我瞪着眼睛密切注视，
队伍远去，火光熄灭。
忽然之间火光又出现，
幻影之城再一次点燃；
向着火热的河谷，
幻影大军威武上路！
告诉我，小小的火花，
行进的军队打算去哪？
着火的是哪一座城市，
在炉中化为灰烬消失！

① flicker ['flikə] v. 闪光

② blazing ['bleiziŋ] a. 燃烧的

③ lustre ['lʌstə] n. 光亮

④ phantom ['fæntəm] n. 幻影

⑤ crumble ['krʌmbl] v. 坍塌

⑥ furnace ['fə:nis] n. 火炉

The Little Land

When at home alone I sit
And am very tired of it,
I have just to shut my eyes
To go sailing through the skies —
To go sailing far away
To the pleasant Land of Play;
To the fairy land afar
Where the Little People are;
Where the clover-tops are trees,
And the rain-pools are the seas,
And the leaves like little ships
Sail about on tiny trips;
And above the daisy tree
Through the grasses,
High o'erhead the **Bumble Bee** [①]
Hums and passes.
In that forest **to and fro** [②]
I can wander, I can go;
See the spider and the fly,

小人国

自己坐在家里面

我感到非常厌倦，

刚刚合上了眼睛，

穿过空中去航行——

要到很远的地方，

到游乐王国；

到遥远的仙境，

那里有小矮人；

三叶草就是林场，

雨中的水塘就是海洋，

树叶就像是小船，

轻飘飘地出海玩；

草丛里，

雏菊花上，

大黄蜂在高处，

嗡嗡飞过。

我在森林中徘徊，

兜来兜去很自在；

看见蜘蛛和苍蝇，

① bumble bee ['bʌmbl'bi:]
  n. 大黄蜂

② to and fro 来回地

And the ants go marching by
Carrying parcels with their feet
Down the green and grassy street.
I can in the **sorrel** ① sit,
Where the **ladybird** ② alit.
I can climb the jointed grass, and on high
See the greater swallows pass in the sky,
And the round sun rolling by
Heeding ③ no such things as I.
Through that forest I can pass
Till, as in a looking glass,
Humming fly and daisy tree
And my tiny self I see,
Painted very clear and neat
On the rain-pool at my feet.
Should a **leaflet** ④ come to land
Drifting near to where I stand,
Straight I'll board that tiny boat
Round the rain-pool sea to float.
Little thoughtful creatures sit
On the grassy coast of it.
Little things with lovely eyes
See me sailing with surprise.
Some are **clad in** ⑤ armour green —
(These have sure to battle been!) —
Some are **pied** ⑥ with every **hue** ⑦,
Black and **crimson** ⑧, gold and blue;
Some have wings and swift are gone;
But they all look kindly on.
When my eyes I once again

① sorrel ['sɔrl] *n.* 酸叶草
② ladybird ['leidibə:d] *n.* 瓢虫

③ heed [hi:d] *v.* 注意，留心

④ leaflet ['li:flət] *n.* 小叶

⑤ clad in 穿着
⑥ pie [pai] *v.* 使杂乱
⑦ hue [hju:] *n.* 色彩
⑧ crimson ['krimzn] *n.* 深红色

还有蚂蚁结队行，

千足扛起那行李，

走过绿绿的草地。

我坐在酸叶草上，

有七星瓢虫发亮。

我爬到草丛上头，

看天上燕子飞走，

一轮太阳忙着转，

这些琐屑无暇管。

穿过树林，

来到小水塘，

就像是穿衣镜，

嗡嗡的苍蝇和雏菊花，

还看见小小的我，

映得清晰又秀气，

若有小舟驶向岸，

停靠在我的身旁，

我会立刻登上船，

到水中漂浮打转。

小动物们心有所想，

坐在青青的岸边。

天真可爱的眼睛，

惊奇地看我远行。

有的身披绿铠甲，

（肯定战后没脱下！）

有的是五颜六色，

黑色、深红、金色和蓝色；

有的插翅飞得快；

他们都关切地看过来。

等我再次睁开眼睛时，

Open, and see all things plain:

High **bare** ① walls, great bare floor;

Great big knobs on drawer and door;

Great big people **perched** ② on chairs,

Stitching ③ **tucks** ④ and mending **tears** ⑤,

Each a hill that I could climb,

And talking nonsense all the time —

O dear me,

That I could be

A sailor on the rain-pool sea,

A climber in the clover tree,

And just come back, a sleepy-head,

Late at night to go to bed.

① bare [beə] *a.* 光秃秃的
② perch [pə:tʃ] *v.* 坐
③ stitch [stitʃ] *v.* 缝
④ tuck [tʌk] *n.* 褶
⑤ tear ['tiə] *n.*（撕破的）
  洞或裂缝

一切清清楚楚在眼前：
高高的墙，地上空荡荡；
大圆把手在抽屉和门上；
大人们坐在椅子上，
缝补衣服很繁忙，
堆得像山那么高，
嘴里胡说八道没完没了——
哦，天哪，
我可以出外呀，
成为池塘里的水手，
爬到三叶草的上头，
深夜入睡的时候，
我才回到这里。

Garden Days

花园时光

Night and Day

When the golden day is done,
Through the closing **portal** ①,
Child and garden, flower and sun,
Vanish all things **mortal** ②.
As the blinding shadows fall,
As the rays **diminish** ③,
Under evening's cloak, they all
Roll away and vanish.
Garden darkened, daisy shut,
Child in bed, they slumber —
Glow-worm ④ in the highway **rut** ⑤,
Mice among the **lumber** ⑥.
In the darkness houses shine,
Parents move with candles;
Till, on all, the night **divine** ⑦
Turns the bedroom handles.
Till at last the day begins
In the east a-breaking,
In the hedges and the **whins** ⑧

夜以继日

① portal ['pɔ:tl] *n.* 大门

② mortal ['mɔ:tl] *a.* 终有一死的

③ diminish [di'miniʃ] *v.* 减少

金色的一天结束，
天色慢慢地变暗，
孩子和花园，花朵和太阳，
什么都不见了。
黑影渐渐地下降，
光线越来越微茫，
在夜幕的笼罩下，
他们都消失不见了。
花园暗下来，雏菊合起来，
小孩在床上，他们睡着了，

④ glow-worm ['gləu'wə:m] *n.* 萤火虫
⑤ rut [rʌt] *n.* 车辙
⑥ lumber ['lʌmbə] *n.* 木材

萤火虫在车辙里藏身，
老鼠在木堆里睡去。
晚上家都很明亮，
大人们端着蜡烛来来回回；
直到深夜的时候，

⑦ divine [di'vain] *a.* 神圣的

卧室的门悄悄合上。
直到天终于变亮，
东方破晓的时光，

⑧ whin [win] *n.* 荆豆

篱笆和荆豆丛里，

Sleeping birds a-waking.

In the darkness shapes of things,

Houses, trees, and hedges,

Clearer grow; and sparrow's wings

Beat on window ledges.

These shall wake the yawing maid;

She the door shall open —

Finding dew on garden **glade** [①]

And the morning broken.

There my garden grows again

Green and rosy painted,

As at eve behind the pane

From my eyes it fainted.

Just as it was shut away,

Toy-like, in the even,

Here I see it glow with day

Under glowing heaven.

Every path and every plot,

Every bush of roses,

Every blue forget-me-not

Where the dew **reposes** [②],

'Up!' they cry, 'the day is come

On the smiling valleys;

We have beat the morning drum;

Playmate, join your allies!'

鸟儿起床活动啦。

黑暗中的那些东西，

房屋、树木和篱笆，

越来越清楚；麻雀的羽翼，

扑腾拍打着窗户。

瞌睡的女仆醒来；

她把房门打开——

露水在那园地上，

又是一个新的早晨。

我的花园又回来啦，

花草重新涂上颜色，

就像傍晚窗外，

花园慢慢褪去色彩。

黄昏的时候，像玩具那样，

花园关在外面，

白天的花园阳光灿烂，

天空很亮。

每条小路每棵树木，

每丛月季，

每朵蓝色勿忘我，

上面都有露珠闪烁，

"起来！"他们喊道，"白天降临

在含笑的河谷上；

我们敲响战鼓，

伙伴，加入队伍！"

① glade [gleid] *n.* 林间空地

② repose [ri'pəuz] *v.* 位于

Nest Eggs

Birds all the sunny day
Flutter and quarrel
Here in the **arbour**①-like
Tent of the laurel.
Here in the fork
The brown nest is seated;
Four little blue eggs
The mother keeps heated.
While we stand watching her,
Staring like gabies,
Safe in each egg are the
Bird's little babies
Soon the frail eggs they shall
Chip, and **upspringing**②
Make all the April woods
Merry with singing.
Younger than we are,
O children, and frailer,
Soon in blue air they'll be

鸟窝里的蛋

① arbour ['ɑ:bə] *n.* 藤架

整整一个艳阳天，
鸟儿扑腾吵不完，
月桂树的营帐，
就像棚架一样，
光秃秃的树上
有棕色的鸟窝；
四只小小的蓝蛋，
妈妈用身体保暖。
我们站着看上面，
傻傻盯着目不转睛，
每颗蛋里，
都有小鸟宝宝。
脆弱的蛋壳就快啄破，
新的生命
让四月的森林里，
充满愉快的歌唱。
小鸟比我们这些孩子，
更小更柔弱，
很快它们就飞上蓝天，

② upspring [ʌp'spriŋ] *v.* 出现

Singer and sailor.
We, so much older,
Taller and stronger,
We shall look down on the
Birdies no longer.
They shall go flying
With musical speeches
High overhead in the
Tops of the **beeches** [1] .
In spite of our wisdom
And sensible talking,
We on our feet must go
Plodding [2] and walking.

歌唱着去远行。
我们比它们年长，
比它们高大强壮，
以后对这些飞鸟，
我们再不能小瞧。
小鸟们将要飞走，
鸣声动听又婉转。
在高高的天上，

① beech [biːtʃ] *n.* 山毛榉

在山毛榉树顶。
虽然我们很聪明，
而且会说得好听，
但是我们用双脚走路，

② plod [plɔd] *v.* 沉重地走

步伐沉重不轻盈。

The Flowers

All the names I know from nurse:
Gardener's **garters** [1], Shepherd's purse,
Bachelor's buttons, Lady's **smock** [2],
And the Lady Hollyhock.
Fairy places, fairy things,
Fairy woods where the wild bee wings,
Tiny trees for tiny dames —
These must all be fairy names!
Tiny woods below whose boughs
Shady fairies weave a house;
Tiny tree-tops, rose or thyme,
Where the braver fairies climb!
Fair are grown-up people's trees,
But the fairest woods are these;
Where if I were not so tall,
I should live for good and all.

花

都是保姆教我认识的花：
花匠的袜带，牧羊人的钱袋，
单身汉的纽扣，女士的罩衣，
还有蜀葵花太太。
童话的世界，神奇的东西，
仙子的森林里野蜂嗡嗡飞，
小花树下有小精灵——
一定都有奇妙的名字！
花木森林的树枝下，
精灵编房子又乘凉；
月季和百里香的小小树顶，
勇敢的精灵会爬上去！
大人的树木好是好，
但是这些树才最好；
如果我不是这么高，
就会一直居住到老。

Summer Sun

Great is the sun, and wide he goes
Through empty heaven without **repose**[1];
And in the blue and glowing days
More thick than rain he showers his rays.
Though closer still the blinds we pull
To keep the shady parlour cool,
Yet he will find a **chink**[2] or two
To slip his golden fingers through.
The dusty **attic**[3], spider-clad,
He, through the keyhole, **maketh**[4] glad;
And through the broken edge of tiles ,
Into the laddered hayloft smiles.
Meantime his golden face around
He bares to all the garden ground,
And sheds a warm and glittering look
Among the ivy's inmost nook.
Above the hills, along the blue
Round the bright air with footing true.
To please the child, to paint the rose,
The gardener of the World, he goes.

夏天的太阳

① repose [ri'pəuz] *n.* 休息

② chink [tʃiŋk] *n.* 裂缝

③ attic ['ætik] *n.* 阁楼

④ maketh *v.*〈古〉make 的
第三人称单数形式

了不起的太阳，轨迹很宽广，

天上不停地运转；

蔚蓝晴朗的天气，

光线比雨丝还浓密。

我们拉下百叶窗，

客厅幽暗又舒爽，

太阳找到一两处缝隙，

把金色的手指往里挤。

尘封的阁楼，蜘蛛结网，

太阳透过钥匙孔，洒上光辉；

穿过破旧的瓦片，

笑眯眯地来到带梯子的干草棚。

太阳金色的脸庞，

把地上的花园照亮，

暖融融的金光闪闪，

照到常春藤的最里面，

山岭上面，沿着大海，

轨迹绕着晴空转。

让孩子满意，为玫瑰上妆，

这位世界园丁正在忙。

The **Dumb**^① Soldier

When the grass was closely **mown**^②,
Walking on the lawn alone,
In the **turf**^③ a hole I found
And hid a soldier underground.
Spring and daisies came **apace**^④;
Grasses hide my hiding-place;
Grasses run like a green sea
O'er the lawn up to my knee.
Under grass alone he lies,
Looking up with leaden eyes,
Scarlet coat and pointed gun,
To the stars and to the sun.
When the grass is ripe like grain,
When the scythe is stoned again,
When the lawn is shaven clear,
Then my hole shall reappear.
I shall find him, never fear,
I shall find my grenadier;
But for all that's gone and come,

不会说话的士兵

① dumb [dʌm] *a.* 哑的，无
   说话能力的
② mown [məun] *v.* (mow
   的过去分词）割
③ turf [tə:f] *n.* 草皮
④ apace [ə'peis] *ad.* 飞快地

草坪仔细修整后，

我独自在上面走，

发现地上有个洞，

里面藏着一个士兵。

春天雏菊花盛开；

草丛遮掩我所在；

草丛像一片绿海，

比草坪高，到我的膝盖。

士兵一人躺下面，

灰色的眼睛望着天，

红色制服，尖尖的枪，

向着星星，向着太阳。

等草长得像稻谷那样，

割草的镰刀又会磨亮，

草坪修剪整洁后，

我的小洞还会有。

我会找到他，别担心，

我会找到士兵；

不管发生什么事，

I shall find my soldier dumb.
He has lived, a little thing,
In the grassy woods of spring;
Done, if he could tell me true,
Just as I should like to do.
He has seen the starry hours
And the springing of the flowers;
And the fairy things that pass
In the forests of the grass.
In the silence he has heard
Talking bee and ladybird,
And the butterfly has flown
O'er him as he lay alone.
Not a word will he **disclose** [1],
Not a word of all he knows.
I must lay him on the shelf,
And make up the tale myself.

我会找到不会说话的士兵。
这个小东西，他就住在，
春天的茂密草地；
如果他能告诉我他的故事，
我也希望如此。
他见过夜色星光，
也见过花朵绽放；
见过小小的仙子
路过茂密的草地。
一片寂静中听到，
蜜蜂瓢虫正在聊，
蝴蝶飞到他上方，
士兵还在独自躺。
一个字也不肯说，
知道的事都沉默。
我要把他放在架子上，
编个故事我自己讲。

① disclose [dis'kləuz] v. 公开，揭露

Autumn Fires

In the other gardens
And all up the vale,
From the autumn bonfires
See the smoke trail!
Pleasant summer over
And all the summer flowers,
The red fire blazes,
The grey smoke **towers** [1].
Sing a song of seasons!
Something bright in all!
Flowers in the summer,
Fires in the fall!

秋日的营火

一座座的花园，
沿着山谷到上面，
秋日的营火里，
看缕缕炊烟升起！
美好的夏天过完，
鲜花都消失不见，
红火焰在燃烧，
灰烟升得很高。
唱一首四季之歌！
歌颂所有的欢乐！
夏天的繁花，
秋日的营火！

① tower ['tauə] v. 高耸

The Gardener

The gardener does not love to talk,
He makes me keep the gravel walk;
And when he puts his tools away;
He locks the door and takes the key.
Away behind the **currant**^① row
Where no one else but cook may go,
Far in the plots, I see him dig,
Old and serious, brown and big.
He digs the flowers, green, red, and blue,
Nor wishes to be spoken to.
He digs the flowers and cuts the hay,
And never seems to want to play.
Silly gardener! summer goes,
And winter comes with **pinching**^② toes,
When in the garden bare and brown
You must lay your **barrow**^③ down.
Well now, and while the summer stays,
To profit by these garden days,
O how much wiser you could be
To play at Indian wars with me!

花匠

① currant ['kʌrnt] *n.* 红醋栗

花匠不太爱说话，

让我守着石子路；

他把工具摆放好，

锁上门拔下钥匙。

那一排醋栗树后，

除了厨师没人会去，

远远地我见他挖土，

年迈而严肃，晒黑的样子很威武。

他挖的野花，颜色各不同，

一声不响不聊天。

挖好野花割干草，

玩耍从来想不到。

② pinch [pintʃ] *v.* 收缩

③ barrow ['bærəu] *n.* 手推车

糊涂的花匠啊！夏天会结束，

冬天踮着脚尖来，

花园光秃秃没有了绿色，

你只好放下手推车。

那么，趁夏天还没走，

好好珍惜花园时光，

和我玩打仗游戏，

那你多么有高见！

Historical Associations^①

Dear Uncle Jim, this garden ground
That now you smoke your pipe around
Has seen **immortal**^② actions done
And **valiant**^③ battles lost and won.
Here we had best on tip-toe tread,
While I for safety march ahead,
For this is that enchanted ground
Where all who **loiter**^④ slumber sound.
Here is the sea, here is the sand,
Here is the simple Shepherd's Land,
Here are the fairy hollyhocks,
And there are Ali Baba's rocks.
But **yonder**^⑤, see! apart and high,
Frozen **Siberia**^⑥ lies; where I,
With Robert Bruce and William Tell,
Was bound by an enchanter's spell.
There, then, awhile in chains we lay,
In wintry **dungeons**^⑦, far from day;
But ris'n at length, with might and main,

历史奇想

① association [əˌsəuʃi'eiʃn] *n.* 联想

② immortal [i'mɔːtl] *a.* 不朽的

③ valiant ['væliənt] *a.* 英勇的

④ loiter ['lɔitə] *v.* 徘徊

⑤ yonder ['jɔndə] *ad.* 在远处

⑥ Silberia [sai'biəriə] *n.* 西伯利亚

⑦ dungeon ['dʌn(d)ʒn] *n.* 地牢

亲爱的吉姆叔叔，就是这个花园，

你正抽着烟斗的地方，

见证过不朽的功绩，

胜败激战在这里。

我们最好踮着脚尖，

安全起见我走在前面，

这可是施过魔法的地盘，

谁要是走散就会有生命危险。

这是大海，这是沙土，

这是牧羊人的家园，

还有神奇的蜀葵

和阿里巴巴的岩石堆。

看呀！高高的那一处地方，

是天寒地冻的西伯利亚；

我和罗伯特还有威廉，

在那里受到巫师的咒语。

那时，睡觉要戴着铁链，

冬日的土牢，黑夜真漫长；

终于爬起来，可真不容易，

Our iron fetters burst in **twain** [①],
Then all the horns were blown in town;
And, to the **ramparts** [②] clanging down,
All the giants leaped to horse
And **charged** [③] behind us through the gorse.
On we rode, the others and I,
Over the mountains blue, and by
The Silent River, the sounding sea,
And the robber woods of **Tartary** [④].
A thousand miles we galloped fast,
And down the witches' lane we passed,
And rode amain, with **brandished** [⑤] sword,
Up to the middle, through the ford.
Last we drew **rein** [⑥] — a weary three —
Upon the lawn, in time for tea,
And from our **steeds** [⑦] alighted down
Before the gates of Babylon.

① twain [twein] *n.* 一对

② rampart ['ræmpɑ:t] *n.* 护城墙

③ charge [tʃɑ:dʒ] *v.* 向……冲去

④ Tartary ['tɑ:təri] *n.* 鞑靼

⑤ brandish ['brændiʃ] *v.* 挥舞

⑥ rein [rein] *n.* 缰绳

⑦ steed [sti:d] *n.* 战马

脚镣咣咣地碰在一起，
城镇的号角全都奏响；
向着城镇，
巨人们都上了马，
冲过金雀花丛追赶。
我们骑着马，三个人一起，
翻过蓝色的山脉，
路过寂静之河与咆哮海洋，
穿过鞑靼强盗的森林。
飞奔了一千英里路，
穿过巫师的小路，
快马奔驰，手挥着剑，
经过浅滩，到达中部。
最后卸下缰绳，三个人很累，
放在草上，赶上茶点时间，
我们从马上下来，
就在巴比伦门前。

Envoys

信

To Willie and Henrietta

If two may read aright
These rhymes of old delight
And house and garden play,
You two, my cousin, and you only, may.

You in a garden green
With me were king and queen,
Were hunter, soldier, **tar** [①],
And all the thousand things that children are.

Now in the elders' seat
We rest with quiet feet,
And from the window-bay
We watch the children, our **successors** [②], play.

'Time was,' the golden head
Irrevocably [③] said;
But time which none can bind,
While flowing fast away, leaves love behind.

致威廉和亨利埃塔

① tar [tɑ:] *n.* 水手

② successor [sək'sesə] *n.* 继承者

③ irrevocably [i'revəkəbli] *ad.* 不可改变地

若世上能有两人理解恰当

这些古老而欢乐的诗行，

以及在房子和花园表演的剧本，

那么两位表兄妹，只有你们能明白。

你们在青青的花园，

和我演国王、王后、

猎人、士兵、水手

和孩子会演的各种各样的角色。

如今在老人的座位，

安安静静坐下休息，

看着窗外，

晚辈孩子们做扮演游戏。

"我们也玩过。"金发老人

说得不容否认；

但谁都留不住时间，

飞逝而过，留下眷恋。

To My Mother

You too, my mother, read my rhymes
For the love of unforgotten times,
And you may chance to hear once more
The little feet along the floor.

致母亲

妈妈呀，你也读读我的诗篇，
为那充满爱的难忘时光而写，
也许你会碰巧再一次听见，
那双小脚轻轻走在地板上。

To Auntie

Chief of our aunts — not only I,
But all your dozen of nurslings cry —
What did the other children do?
And what were childhood, **wanting** [①] *you?*

致阿姨

① want [wɔnt] v. 缺少

园长阿姨，不是我一个人吵，
十几个小孩都在哭闹，
其他孩子小时候怎么过？
没有你，我们哪里还有童年？

To Minnie

The red room with the giant bed
Where none but elders laid their head;
The little room where you and I
Did for awhile together lie
And, simple **suitor** ①, I your hand
In decent marriage did demand;
The great day nursery, best of all,
With pictures pasted on the wall
And leaves upon the blind —
A pleasant room wherein to wake
And hear the leafy garden shake
And **rustle** ② in the wind —
And pleasant there to lie in bed
And see the pictures overhead —
The wars about **Sebastopol** ③,
The grinning guns along the wall,
The daring **escalade** ④,
The **plunging** ⑤ ships, the bleating sheep,
The happy children ankle-deep

致米妮

① suitor ['suːtə] *n.* 求婚者

② rustle ['rʌsl] *n.* 沙沙声

③ Sebastopol [si'bæstəpəul] *n.* 塞巴斯托波（美国地名）

④ escalade [ˌeskə'leid] *v.* 架起梯子攻击

⑤ plunge [plʌndʒ] *v.*（轮船）颠簸

红色房间的大床，

只有长辈才会去躺；

小房间里我和你，

真的曾经躺在一起，

求爱者牵你的手，

真的希望到白头；

育儿室里最好玩，

墙上贴满图画，

百叶窗拉上——

这是睡醒的好地方，

听到花园里的树在摇摆，

沙沙作响有风吹来；

躺在床上很惬意，

看看上面的画——

塞巴斯托波尔大战，

墙边闪亮的枪支，

勇猛地架梯子攻城，

颠簸的轮船，咩咩叫的羊，

和脚踝一般高的孩子很开心，

And laughing as they **wade**①;

All these are vanished clean away,

And the old **manse**② is changed to-day;

It wears an altered face

And shields a stranger race.

The river, on from mill to mill,

Flows past our childhood's garden still;

But ah! we children never more

Shall watch it from the water-door!

Below the **yew**③ — it still is there —

Our phantom voices haunt the air

As we were still at play,

And I can hear them call and say:

'How far is it to Babylon?'

Ah, far enough, my dear,

Far, far enough from here —

Yet you have farther gone!

'Can I get there by candlelight?'

So goes the old **refrain**④,

I do not know — **perchance**⑤ you might —

But only, children, hear it right,

Ah, never to return again!

The eternal dawn, beyond a doubt,

Shall break on hill and plain,

And put all stars and candles out,

Ere we be young again.

To you in distant India, these

I send across the seas,

Nor count it far across.

For which of us forgets

① wade [weid] *v.* 跋涉

② manse [mæns] *n.* 牧师住宅

③ yew [ju:] *n.* 紫杉

④ refrain [ri'frein] *n.* 叠句
⑤ perchance [pə'tʃɑ:ns] *ad.* 也许

大步走着嘻嘻哈哈。

现在一切都不见，

老房子已经改变，

换了不同的容颜，

守护陌生的家园。

小河，连着一座座磨坊，

还经过儿时的花园流淌；

可是！我们再也没机会

去水闸看看河水！

杉树还在老地方，

我们的声音在树下回荡，

仿佛我们还在做游戏，

还能听到他们问：

"到巴比伦有多远？"

亲爱的，很遥远，

离这里非常非常远，

不过你已经走得很远！

"能不能在烛光中走到那里？"

这是旧歌谣里的说法，

我不知道，也许可以，

但是孩子，听仔细，

永远不要再回家！

永久的黎明必然

在山丘平原上出现，

星星灯烛都暗淡，

我们不会回到从前。

把这些给远在印度的你，

漂洋过海地寄过去，

距离再远也要给你。

我们谁会忘记，

The Indian cabinets,

The bones of **antelope**[①], the wings of **albatross**[②].

The pied and painted birds and beans,

The **junks**[③] and **bangles**[④], **beads**[⑤] and **screens**[⑥],

The gods and **sacred**[⑦] bells,

And the loud-humming, twisted shells?

The level of the parlour floor

Was honest, homely, Scottish shore;

But when we climbed upon a chair,

Behold the gorgeous East was there!

Be this a **fable**[⑧]; and behold

Me in the parlour as of old,

And Minnie just above me set

In the **quaint**[⑨] Indian cabinet!

Smiling and kind, you grace a shelf

Too high for me to reach myself.

Reach down a hand, my dear, and take

These rhymes **for** old acquaintance' **sake**[⑩].

① antelope ['æntiləup] *n.* 羚羊
② albatross ['ælbətrɔs] *n.* 信天翁
③ junk [dʒʌŋk] *n.* 杂物
④ bangle ['bæŋgl] *n.* 镯子
⑤ bead [bi:d] *n.* 珠子
⑥ screen [skri:n] *n.* 帘子
⑦ sacred ['seikrid] *a.* 神圣的

⑧ fable ['feibl] *n.* 神奇的故事

⑨ quaint [kweint] *a.* 新奇有趣的

⑩ for sb's sake 看在……的分上

印度的柜子，
羚羊的骨头，信天翁的羽翼。
涂成彩色的鸟儿和豆子，
杂物手镯，珠子帘子，
神像和铃铛，
回声很响的海螺壳？
客厅里的地面，
是朴实温馨的苏格兰港湾；
我们爬到椅子上，
一睹瑰丽的东方！
就当是一个童话；
我还是待在客厅，
米妮在上面，
在别致的印度柜子里！
你在上面笑意和善，
架子太高我够不着。
亲爱的，递下手来，给你
这些诗行，不负老朋友一场。

To My Name-Child

1

Some day soon this rhyming **volume**^①, if you learn with proper speed,
Little Louis Sanchez, will be given you to read.
Then shall you discover, that your name was printed down
By the English printers, long before, in London town.
In the great and busy city where the East and West are met,
All the little letters did the English printers set;
While you thought of nothing, and were still too young to play,
Foreign people thought of you in places far away.
Ay, and while you slept, a baby, over all the English lands
Other little children took the volume in their hands;
Other children **questioned**^②, in their homes across the seas:
Who was Little Louis, won't you tell us, mother, please?

2

Now that you have spelt your lesson, lay it down and go and play.
Seeking shells and seaweed on the sands of **Monterey**^③,

致和我同名的小孩

1

① volume ['vɔlju:m] n. 一本，一册

小路易斯，如果你踏实学习，
不久后这卷诗，将送到你手里。
你发现，很久以前的伦敦，
打印机已经把你的名字印成字。
在这座东西交会的繁华都市，
英国打印机印下所有的字词；
你还不懂事，还不会做游戏，
外国的人们在远方想着你。
小宝宝，你睡在英国的领地，
别的小朋友手捧着这部诗集；

② question ['kwestʃən] v. 询问

在海外的家里，他们想知道：
谁是小路易斯？妈妈，告诉我们好不好？

2

③ Monterey [mɔntə'rei] n. 蒙特利（美国城市）

背完了课文，放下书本出去玩吧。
去蒙特利的沙滩，找些贝壳海藻，

Watching all the mighty **whalebones** ⓵, lying buried by the breeze,

Tiny **sandy-pipers** ⓶, and the huge Pacific seas.

And remember in your playing, as the sea-fog rolls to you,

Long are you could read it, how I told you what to do;

And that while you thought of no one, nearly half the world away

Some one thought of Louis on the beach of Monterey!

① whalebone ['weilbəun] *n.*
鲸须
② sandy-piper
['sændi'paipə] *n.* 鹬

看巨大的鲸鱼，风中躺在海里，
渺小的鹬鸟，辽阔的太平洋。
你玩耍的时候，海雾席卷而来，
等读到后面，我会教你如何对待；
你谁也没想，在地球的另一边，
有人却想象路易斯在蒙特利沙滩！

To Any Reader

As from the house your mother sees
You playing round the garden trees,
So you may see, if you will look
Through the windows of this book,
Another child, far, far away,
And in another garden, play.
But do not think you can at all,
By knocking on the window, call
That child to hear you. He intent
Is all on his play-business bent.
He does not hear; he will not look,
Nor yet be lured out of his book.
For, long ago, the truth to say,
He has grown up and gone away,
And it is but a child of air
That **lingers** [1] in the garden there.

致读者

就像妈妈在家里看你
绕着花园的树玩游戏，
如果透过这本书的窗户看去，
你会看见
远处的另一个小孩
在另一座花园里玩耍。
可别以为敲敲窗户，
你就可以让他听见你。
他全神贯注，
一心只想着做游戏。
他听不到，看不到，
不会从书里走出来。
其实很久以前，
他已长大走远，
他只是一个幻影小孩，
留在花园里舍不得离开。

① linger ['liŋgə] v. 逗留